Bubb

Mary's mum a[...]
Bubble and Squeak stay out in the cold
if they get dirty once more. They're
fed-up with puppy pawprints all over
the house!

Mary's sad but the two naughty pups
love playing in the mud. How can she
teach them to keep clean?

Banger and Mash

Mia is going to decorate her bedroom
and puppy twins, Banger and Mash
can't wait to help. But Mia's mum
thinks that paws and paint are a recipe
for mess.

Will the pups be allowed to join in the
fun?

Titles in Jenny Dale's PUPPY TALES™ series

All of Jenny Dale's PUPPY TALES™ books can
be ordered at your local bookshop or are
available by post from Book Service by Post
(tel: 01624 675737)

Jenny Dale's PUPPY TALES™

A Puppy Tales™ Twins Two-Books-in-One Special!

Bubble and Squeak
Banger and Mash

Jenny Dale

Illustrated by Susan Hellard

A Working Partners Book
MACMILLAN CHILDREN'S BOOKS

Special thanks to Narinder Dhami

Bubble and Squeak first published 2001 by Macmillan Children's Books
Banger and Mash first published 2001 by Macmillan Children's Books

This edition first published 2001 by Macmillan Children's Books
a division of Pan Macmillan Limited
20 New Wharf Road, London N1 9RR
Basingstoke and Oxford
www.panmacmillan.com

Associated companies throughout the world

Created by Working Partners Limited
London W6 0QT

ISBN 0 330 39994 2

3 5 7 9 8 6 4

A CIP catalogue record for this book is available from
the British Library.

Typeset by SX Composing DTP, Rayleigh, Essex
Printed and bound in Great Britain by Mackays of Chatham plc, Kent

Bubble and Squeak

To the real Mary Connor – a true friend

Chapter One

"Come on, Squeak!" Bubble barked, as he splashed about in the foamy bubbles. "The water's lovely!"

"I don't want a bath," Squeak whined, his ears flat against his head. He backed into a corner and tried to make himself as small as possible.

"Look at the pair of you – you're both filthy." Mary Connor, the pups' owner, was pouring dog shampoo over Bubble's muddy back. "You look more like two brown dogs than two white ones!"

"We were only playing, Mary," Bubble woofed, snapping at a bubble that floated up into the air. "We rolled in the mud, and we had a *great* time!"

"But now we've got to have another horrible *bath*," Squeak whimpered. Miserably, he plumped down on his fat little bottom and put his head on his paws. It was all right for Bubble – he loved baths. Squeak hated them even more than he hated going to the vet!

"I hope I can get you both clean before Dad sees you," Mary said, looking worried. She lifted Bubble out and began to dry him with an old towel.

"Yes, Squeak, we don't want Mr Connor to see that we've got dirty *again*," Bubble yapped anxiously. "You know he doesn't like it."

Squeak's heart sank. He knew Bubble was right. He'd have to have a bath, or Mr Connor would be cross. Mary's dad didn't think Bubble and Squeak were the right sort of dogs to live on a busy farm. Until a few weeks ago, the puppy twins had lived in a house with their mum, Molly, and her owner, Mr Nolan. Then Mary had

arrived to collect them with her
mum and dad . . .

"Oh, they're gorgeous!" Mary
said.

  Bubble and Squeak rushed over
to meet her, their tails wagging.
Mary's voice was soft, and she
handled the pups gently when
she stroked them.

  "She's nice!" Squeak woofed.

"I like her!" Bubble barked.

Mrs Connor looked nice too.

But Mr Connor stood there frowning. "They're *white*," he said. "I thought they'd be brown, like Molly."

Mr Nolan shrugged. "Well, they're the only ones left from the litter."

Bubble and Squeak looked at each other, then crept away to hide behind their mum. They weren't sure why Mr Connor didn't like their white coats.

"With all the rain and mud they'll be filthy the whole time," Mr Connor went on.

"Oh, Dad," Mary said. She picked the pups up, hugging one in each arm. "I'll keep them clean.

I'll bath them whenever they need it!"

"Bath?" Squeak gave a puzzled woof. "What's that?"

"They *are* very cute, John," Mary's mum added.

Mr Connor sighed, and nodded his head.

"Thanks, Dad!" Mary cried. She rushed over to kiss him, still carrying the two pups . . .

The trouble was, Mr Connor was right, Squeak thought. It *was* difficult for him and his brother to stay clean on the farm. There were just too many tempting puddles and muddy fields and damp ditches!

And when they got muddy,

Mary had to bath them in the big outhouse sink before they were allowed into the kitchen.

"Come on, Squeak," Mary said, as she finished drying Bubble. "It's your turn now."

"No-o-o-o!" Squeak howled as Mary bent to pick him up.

Just then, the outhouse door opened. Squeak's eyes lit up. This was his chance! He wriggled away from Mary, and made a dash for it.

Mary and Bubble jumped up to chase after him, and Mary knocked the soapdish flying.

"Oh no, you don't, Squeak!" A firm hand grasped the scruff of Squeak's neck, just as he reached the doorway. "Here's the little rascal, Mary." Mr Connor handed a whimpering Squeak over to his daughter. "And make sure he doesn't get away this time – aaargh!"

Mary's dad slipped on the bar of soap, which had fallen to the floor. He skidded forward, and went head-first into the sink full of bubbles.

Chapter Two

Mr Connor wiped the suds from his face. "I *knew* these two pups would be trouble!" he shouted crossly.

"Sorry, Dad!" Mary cried. "I knocked the soapdish over when Squeak escaped."

"Well, either they keep clean

from now on, or they'll have to live outside – and I mean it this time!" Mr Connor stomped off across the farmyard.

Squeak looked at Bubble in dismay. Mr Connor sounded really serious. And now Mary was in trouble too. "OK, I'll have a bath now," he whimpered. "But we'd better not get mucky tomorrow."

"What shall we do today, then, Bubble?" Squeak yapped.

It was the following morning. Mary was eating breakfast before going to school. The puppies were waiting hopefully for titbits under the kitchen table.

"We could chase the ducks

around the farmyard," Bubble woofed, wagging his tail cheerfully. "And then we could go into the field and find some lovely cowpats to roll in. And then we could find a big puddle and—"

"No, no, *no!*" Squeak barked. "You heard what Mr Connor said. He'll make us live outside if we get dirty again so soon."

"But we're dogs – and dogs *like* getting dirty," Bubble pointed out.

"I know." Squeak nipped his brother's ear playfully. "But Mr Connor doesn't like it."

"So?" Bubble jumped on Squeak. "Mr Connor isn't very clean himself after he's worked on the farm all day, is he? He stinks!"

"But at least Mr Connor likes having baths," Squeak panted, as he and Bubble rolled over and over underneath the table. "*I* don't! So let's try and keep clean from now on," he growled, pinning Bubble to the ground.

"What are those two up to?" Mr Connor peered under the table.

"They're just playing, Dad," Mary laughed, as the two pups sat up and shook themselves.

"Would you hurry up, Mary, and finish your breakfast, please?" Mrs Connor said. "You too, John."

"But, Bridie, I've only just sat down to my bacon and eggs!" Mary's dad said grumpily.

"Well, I have to get on with the cleaning, John," said Mrs Connor. "This house is a terrible mess."

Mary and her father looked at each other. "Mrs Riley!" they groaned.

Mary's mum looked flustered. "Well, yes, Mrs Riley *is* coming to visit this afternoon."

"Great! Mrs Riley!" Bubble woofed. "She brought a yummy cake last time, and dropped lots of crumbs!"

"I remember!" Squeak woofed back. "I wonder what she'll bring this time?"

"Not that woman again," Mary's dad grumbled. "All she does is boast about how much money she's got."

"And she's really snooty too,"
Mary added, slipping two bits of
toast under the table.

"Hey, you nicked the biggest
bit!" Bubble yapped, as Squeak
wolfed it down.

"Well, she *is* a neighbour,"
Mrs Connor muttered. She began
to wipe the kitchen table.

"Can I finish my breakfast
before you wipe my plate?"
Mary's dad said, as Mrs Connor
picked up his plate of bacon and
eggs and wiped the table
underneath it.

"Mum, will you keep Bubble
and Squeak inside today, please?"
Mary asked. She picked up her
schoolbag. "I don't want them
getting dirty again."

"Yes, but they'd better not get under my feet," Mrs Connor said. "I'm going to be very busy."

"I don't want to stay inside," Squeak whined as he and Bubble went to see Mary safely out of the house, as they did every morning.

"Bye, Bubble. Bye, Squeak." Mary kissed each pup in turn. "Be good!"

"At least we'll keep clean if we stay inside, Squeak," Bubble pointed out.

Squeak wagged his tail more cheerfully. "That's true."

"And there are loads of games we can play inside," Bubble woofed. "Come on, let's go and play *Hide-Mr-Connor's-slippers*!"

The pups raced each other up

the stairs.

But Mrs Connor had got there before them, and was dusting the bedroom furniture. "Out!" she said crossly.

Bubble and Squeak whined as Mrs Connor shut the door, leaving them on the landing.

"I know," Squeak barked. "Let's go and play *Hide-under-Mary's-rug!*"

That was one of their favourite games. One of the pups would crawl under the rug on Mary's bedroom floor, while the other one pounced on him every time he moved. It was great fun.

But not for long. The pups had hardly started their game before Mrs Connor bustled in with her duster.

"Out you go!" she said briskly.

"It's not fair!" Squeak complained, but Mrs Connor put them outside, and closed the door *again*.

It was the same all morning. Whenever the pups tried to play a quiet game of *Chew-the-bathmat* or *Running-up-and-down-the-stairs-very-fast*, Mrs Connor put a stop to it.

"We can't do *anything*," Squeak whined as they sat in the hall. They'd been shut out of every single room in the farmhouse.

"Well, maybe we could *help* Mrs Connor instead of playing games," Bubble woofed. "Look!"

Mrs Connor was battling with some kind of monster which had been hiding in the cupboard under the stairs. Bubble and Squeak both growled and bared their teeth. She would *definitely* need their help now. It was their duty to protect Mary and her family from this big, noisy monster!

"Grrr! We're ready for you!" Bubble barked. He dashed down the hall towards Mrs Connor. "I'll bark at you until you stop making that horrible noise!"

"And I'll bite you!" Squeak growled. He grabbed one end of the monster and hung onto it as Mrs Connor tried to push it along.

"Right, that's it! I can't even hoover in peace," Mrs Connor said crossly. She stormed over to the back door and opened it. "Outside – NOW!"

The pups trailed gloomily out into the farmyard.

"Doesn't Mrs Connor know we're trying to help?" Bubble yapped, as he sniffed the air. It had been raining, and everything smelled cool and damp.

"Remember what we said about keeping clean, Bubble!" Squeak

woofed anxiously. The farmyard was awash with mud, and there were lots of puddles.

"Oh, yes . . ." Bubble's eyes lit up. He'd noticed a really *big* puddle, right next to them.

"We don't want to live outside in a kennel, do we?" Squeak reminded him.

"No," Bubble agreed. But the puddle looked so deep, he just *had* to jump right into the middle of it – and he splashed Squeak from head to toe.

"You did that on purpose!" Squeak whined as Bubble ran off, barking gleefully.

Squeak chased his brother through every puddle in the farmyard. Soon, both pups were soaked and filthy. They headed off into one of the fields, where Bubble found some even thicker mud to roll around in. It had been churned up by Mr Connor's tractor.

"I'm hungry!" Squeak whined when they were covered in mud from head to toe.

"So am I," woofed Bubble. He headed back to the farmhouse. Squeak followed.

As usual, the back door was propped open. The two pups charged into the kitchen, leaving muddy pawprints on the clean floor.

Bubble stopped and sniffed the air. "I can smell someone different," he yapped. "Mrs Riley must be here!"

Squeak didn't reply. He was too busy stealing a dog biscuit from Bubble's bowl.

"Hey, I was saving that for later," Bubble barked crossly. Squeak took to his heels, still carrying the biscuit in his mouth, and headed for the living room.

A woman in posh clothes sat on the sofa next to Mrs Connor. It was Mrs Riley. She looked around the room and sniffed snootily. "It must be *very* difficult, trying to keep things clean on a farm," she said. "I do feel sorry for you, Bridie."

Mrs Connor went a bit red. "Oh, it's not too bad," she said.

Mrs Riley looked at Mary's mum. "You should see *my* house," she said. "It's spotless. But then, of course, I *do* have a cleaner and a housekeeper."

"More tea?" Mrs Connor asked grumpily, picking up the tea tray. "I'll just pop out to the kitchen and put the kettle on again."

Right at that moment Squeak barged into the living room, followed by Bubble. Mrs Connor was just behind the door, and the tray was knocked right out of her hands.

"Oh!" Mrs Connor gasped as everything crashed to the floor.

Bubble and Squeak didn't even notice. They were too busy greeting the visitor.

"Have you brought anything nice to eat?" Bubble barked. "That

cake you brought last time was yummy!" He jumped up at Mrs Riley and left muddy pawprints all over her cream skirt.

"I bet there's something nice in here!" Squeak yapped. He stuck his nose into Mrs Riley's big shiny handbag. He was so excited, he dropped the dog biscuit inside it.

"Help!" Mrs Riley screamed. "Get these filthy little dogs away from me!"

Chapter Three

"It was your fault for jumping in that puddle, Squeak!" Bubble whined.

"No, it was *yours* for finding all that lovely mud to roll in!" Squeak whimpered.

The puppies were in disgrace.

Mrs Riley had stormed out of

the farmhouse, and Mary's mum had had to clean up all the mess. But first she'd shut the pups in an empty pig-pen.

"And you can stay there till Mary comes home from school!" Mrs Connor had said crossly, slamming the door shut.

Bubble and Squeak huddled together in a corner of the smelly pen, feeling very worried. What would Mary say when she saw them? What would Mr Connor say?

"Don't worry, Squeak." Bubble licked his brother's nose. "Mary will give us a bath, and everything will be OK."

"*Another* bath," Squeak whined. He shivered.

Suddenly Bubble sat up and sniffed the air. "It's Mary!" he barked.

A moment later, Mary popped her head over the side of the pen. "Look at you two!" she said. "You're both filthy, and Mum's really angry."

Bubble and Squeak huddled together sadly, their stumpy tails between their legs.

Mary sighed, shaking her head. Then she let herself into the pen and picked them both up for a cuddle.

Bubble licked her ear. "We're very sorry, Mary," he woofed softly.

"At least *you* don't mind if we're dirty or not," Squeak whimpered as he snuffled his nose into Mary's neck.

Mr and Mrs Connor came out into the farmyard. They both looked furious. Bubble and Squeak's hearts sank.

"Put those pups down, Mary!" Mrs Connor said sharply. "You'll get your school clothes dirty."

Mary quickly put Bubble and Squeak down on the ground. "I'm really sorry about what happened, Mum," she said.

"I've never been so embarrassed in my life," Mrs Connor went on. "And in front of Mrs Riley too."

"This is their last chance, Mary," Mr Connor said sternly. "If the pups can't keep themselves clean, they really will have to live outside in a kennel. And they won't be allowed in the house at all. I've had enough."

Bubble and Squeak looked at each other and whimpered. They didn't want to live in a horrible old kennel. They wanted to be with Mary in the farmhouse. They wanted to sleep on Mary's bed. And sit under the kitchen table waiting for titbits. And curl up in front of the fire in the living room – like they always did.

As Mary went off to fill the outhouse sink with water, Squeak yapped at his brother. "Bubble, we've just *got* to keep clean from now on."

"I know," Bubble yapped in

agreement. "Don't worry, it'll be easy!"

But it *wasn't* easy. It rained a lot – and that made the farmyard even muddier. Mary helped all she could. When she took Bubble and Squeak out for their morning walk, she carried them over the muddiest puddles. But she couldn't help when she was at school.

"Mind that puddle, Squeak!" Bubble barked, as they took a stroll around the farmyard the following afternoon.

Squeak tiptoed carefully round it. He couldn't help staring at the puddle as he did so. He was longing to jump in and splash around. But he knew Mary would be upset, so he didn't.

"Yaaah! Can't catch me!" One of the ducks scurried past on its way to the pond, quacking loudly.

Bubble was about to chase after it when Squeak grabbed his tail.

"No, Bubble!" he barked. "Look at the mud around the pond!"

Bubble growled a bit, then gave up on the duck-chasing idea.

The two pups raced back into the farmhouse, where it was a lot safer.

At least, they *thought* they were safe.

While Bubble was sniffing around the big open fireplace, a shower of soot fell down the chimney. It nearly covered him in black dust. Luckily, Bubble jumped out of the way, just in time.

"We can't go *anywhere* or do *anything*!" Squeak yapped. "There's dirt all over the place!"

"But just think how happy Mary will be that we're still white!" Bubble barked.

And he was right. Mary was

really pleased when she came home from school and saw her two clean puppies. "Well done, boys!" she cried, giving them both a hug.

But Bubble and Squeak couldn't help feeling worried. This was only the first day, and it had been *really* difficult. How on earth were they going to keep it up?

Chapter Four

"Bubble and Squeak have been
very good, haven't they, Mum?"
Mary asked proudly.

She was sitting with her mum in
the living room, watching TV. The
pups were curled up together in
one big fluffy white ball on her
lap. "They've stayed clean for a

whole week."

"And it was really difficult too," Bubble yapped.

"But at least it means no baths!" Squeak woofed.

The pups had spent most of their time playing and sleeping in Mary's bedroom, where they felt safe. It was very boring staying inside all the time, but at least they hadn't got dirty.

Mrs Connor put her knitting down as the programme finished, and the adverts began. "Well, let's hope it lasts," she said. "I'll go and put the kettle on. Your dad should be home from the market soon."

"I bet you're the first one to get dirty!" Squeak yapped. He gave his brother a little nip.

"No, I bet *you* are!" Bubble nipped him back, and they started rolling around together on Mary's lap.

"New Kleener-than-Kleen's wonderful *bubbles* will make your hair *squeaky* clean!" said a loud voice.

Bubble and Squeak stopped rolling around and sat up, their ears pricked.

"Someone said our names!" Bubble barked.

"Who was it?" Squeak yapped.

Mary was laughing. "Look, Mum!" she said, as Mrs Connor paused in the doorway. "The pups heard their names on the TV!"

Bubble and Squeak knew what

the TV was. It was that strange box in the corner of the room that had lots of people and sometimes even other dogs inside it. They stared at the screen.

A woman was shaking her long hair around, and holding a big green bottle. "It's true!" she said. "*Kleener-than-Kleen*'s bubbles really *do* make your hair squeaky clean!"

Bubble and Squeak began to bark when they heard their names again. "She's talking about us!"

Mary grinned. "Maybe we should get some *Kleener-than-Kleen* shampoo for Bubble and Squeak!" she joked. "Not that they need it," she added quickly, as her mum frowned. "They're being so good at the moment. They're already cleaner-than-clean!"

Bubble and Squeak looked at each other proudly. They were cleaner-than-clean! That wasn't bad for two pups who had been in trouble for being filthy just a week ago. Now all they had to do was keep it up . . .

"I hope you boys are going to be

careful," Mrs Connor said with a frown. She was pegging out some washing, a few days later. The sun had come out – but it had been raining for hours and hours, and the farmyard was full of muddy puddles.

"Of *course* we're going to be careful!" Bubble sniffed, as Mrs Connor picked up the washing-basket and went inside.

"What shall we do now?" Squeak woofed.

"Let's wait by the gate for Mary to come home from school," Bubble yapped back.

"OK," Squeak agreed.

But as they were making their way over to the gate, something happened. A huge gust of wind blew across the farmyard. It tugged a yellow T-shirt off the washing-line and carried it away.

Bubble didn't notice, but Squeak did. "Oh no!" he barked. "That's Mary's favourite T-shirt!"

Determined to get the T-shirt back, Squeak chased after it. Splash! He ran through one muddy puddle. Splash! And another.

"Squeak! Be careful!" Bubble yelped, horrified.

Suddenly the wind died down for a moment and the T-shirt fell to the ground.

Squeak rushed towards it through the mud. He grabbed it in his teeth. "Goth ith!" he woofed. It was hard to woof with T-shirt in his mouth.

"And the mud's got *you*!" Bubble whined, rushing over to him. "Squeak, you're *filthy*!"

Chapter Five

Squeak looked down at himself. He *was* dirty. In fact, he was dirtier-than-dirty! He dropped the T-shirt back on the ground. "Bubble, what are we going to do?" he whimpered. "If Mr and Mrs Connor see me like this, we'll never be allowed in the house again."

"And Mary will be really upset,"
Bubble added. Then his ears
perked up and his tail started to
wag. "I've got a brilliant idea!"

Squeak's ears perked up too.
"What?" he asked.

"*I'll* bath you!" Bubble barked.

"Oh no!" Squeak lay his ears flat
against his head and backed away
from his brother. "No way!" he
woofed.

"Have you got any better
ideas?" Bubble yapped sternly.

Squeak looked glum. "No," he
sniffed.

"Come on, then," Bubble
woofed. He turned and headed
off towards the stables on the
other side of the farmyard.

Squeak picked up Mary's T-shirt

and followed his brother.

"We can't bath you in the outhouse sink," Bubble woofed as he ran, "because we can't turn the taps on. But I know where there is some water already poured."

He stopped by one of the troughs that were full of drinking water for the horses. "You'll have to have a bath in there!"

Squeak dropped the T-shirt again,

then howled. "But that's for the *horses*. And anyway, you can't bath me – you haven't got any soap!"

Bubble cocked his head to one side. "You're right, Squeak," he woofed. "I'll go and get some." He dashed off towards the house.

Mrs Connor was on the phone when Bubble sneaked in, so she didn't see him run up the stairs into the bathroom.

Panting, Bubble stopped and looked around. He couldn't see the doggy soap Mary always used when she bathed them. But there was a big green bottle on the side of the bath. Bubble had seen that same bottle on the TV. It was *Kleener-than-Kleen*! Mrs Connor must have bought it when she went shopping the day before.

Perfect, Bubble thought. He grabbed the bottle in his teeth, and hurried outside again.

Squeak was waiting by the horse trough, shivering.

Bubble dropped the bottle on the ground. "Help me get the top off, Squeak," he yapped.

First Squeak tucked Mary's T-shirt safely under the trough where it couldn't blow away again. Then Bubble held the bottle between his paws while Squeak twisted the top off with his teeth.

"In you get, Squeak," Bubble yapped firmly after he'd tipped a drop of shampoo into the trough.

"Do I *have* to?" Squeak whimpered.

"Yes, you do!" Bubble barked. Then he took another look at his brother. Squeak really was FILTHY! He tipped some more shampoo into the trough. This time half the bottle went in. "Come on, Mary will be home from school soon," he added.

Slowly, Squeak climbed into the trough. "Ooh! It's fre-e-e-zing!" he howled as the cold water touched his tummy.

"Make sure you roll about and get all the dirt off," Bubble yapped.

Shivering, Squeak began to roll about in the water. But, all of a sudden, something happened! Bubbles began to appear. Hundreds and hundreds – and HUNDREDS of them. And they kept on coming.

The bubbles began to cover Squeak completely. "Help!" he spluttered. "Help! There's a Bubble Monster in here, and he's attacking me!"

"Oh no!" Bubble yelped, as Squeak disappeared under a mound of bubbles. "What am I going to do? I've *got* to save Squeak from the Bubble Monster."

Chapter Six

The bubbles in the trough were
getting higher and higher, and
foamier and foamier all the time.

"Don't worry, Squeak!" Bubble
barked. "I'll get help!" He shot
away across the farmyard,
splashing through all the puddles
and the thick mud. He was about

to run towards the house. But suddenly he spotted Mary and her mum walking down the lane. Mrs Connor must have gone to meet Mary from school, and they were almost home.

"Mary!" Bubble barked at the top of his voice, sticking his head through the gate. "Mary, come quick! The Bubble Monster's attacking Squeak, and I don't know what to do!"

"Bubble!" Mary ran towards him. "What's the matter? Where's Squeak?"

"Quick!" Bubble danced around Mary's ankles as she came through the gate. "Follow me!" And he dashed back to the stables.

Mary and Mrs Connor followed.

They stopped and stared when they saw the horse trough absolutely overflowing with bubbles. There was so much foam that Squeak was nowhere to be seen.

"What's happened?" Mary asked, looking confused. But just then a little head appeared from the middle of the bubbles.

"Mary!" Squeak whimpered. "Save me!"

"It's Squeak!" Mary cried, and hurried to the rescue. She plunged her arms into the trough, and pulled the little dog out. Squeak was covered in foam and couldn't stop sneezing.

"Squeak, are you all right?" Bubble barked.

Just then, Mr Connor brought one of the horses into the stables. "What on earth's going on here?" he said.

Bubble whined. In his dash to get help for Squeak, he had got rather muddy himself.

Squeak snuggled even closer to Mary and buried his wet, foamy face in her shoulder. They'd had their very last chance now, and Mr Connor would make them live outside in a cold kennel from now on.

"Look!" Mary noticed the bottle of shampoo lying on the ground. "Bubble, were you trying to bath Squeak because he'd got dirty?"

"You're not telling me those pups have been trying to bath

themselves?" Mr Connor said. Then he burst out laughing.

"I think they have!" said Mrs Connor. She was smiling too.

"It's not funny!" Squeak barked crossly, still clinging to Mary. "I was nearly eaten by the Bubble Monster!"

Mary picked up the bottle. "No wonder there were so many bubbles," she grinned. "This is *Extra-Foamy-Kleener-than-Kleen*!"

Her mum and dad laughed even harder.

"I wonder how Squeak managed to get so dirty in the first place," Mary said. Then she spotted something yellow tucked underneath the trough. She put Squeak down and picked it up.

"It's my T-shirt!"

"I hung that out on the line this afternoon," Mrs Connor said. "What's it doing there?"

Mary gasped. "Maybe it blew away and Squeak rescued it!" she said. "That could be why he's dirty! And maybe Bubble got muddy when he ran for help."

"These two are a right pair!" said Mr Connor. He was still roaring with laughter. "You never know what they're going to get up to next!"

Bubble and Squeak's hopes rose. Mr Connor wasn't angry. And Mrs Connor wasn't either. Maybe the pups hadn't lost their last chance after all.

"Dad, Mum, you're not going

to make Bubble and Squeak live outside now, are you?" Mary asked.

Two pairs of big brown eyes stared at Mr and Mrs Connor. Bubble and Squeak waited to hear what they would say.

"Well . . ." Mr Connor looked down at the pups. "I've kind of got used to having them around the house. I think I'd miss them if they lived outside." He looked at Mary's mum.

Mrs Connor thought for a while. "If the pups did come into the house, Mrs Riley would never visit us again," she said. Then she grinned. "But really, I don't care at all! I've had enough of that Mrs Riley's snooty ways!" She turned to Mary. "So as long as Bubble and Squeak stay clean for *most* of the time, they can live inside," she agreed.

"Yes!" Bubble woofed happily. "Squeak, we don't have to live outside in a horrible old kennel!"

"Brilliant!" Squeak barked, and wriggled to be let down.

Mary put Squeak back on the ground, and the two pups raced around in circles, chasing each other's tails. Everything had worked out fine.

"Hey, Squeak!" Bubble playfully nipped his brother's ear and then ran off. "*Kleener-than-Kleen* really does make you SQUEAKY clean then!"

"That's an awful joke, Bubble!"

Squeak woofed, chasing his brother across the farmyard.

"Mind the puddles, boys!" Mary called after them.

Bubble and Squeak had stopped right on the edge of a big puddle of very dirty water.

"Mrs Connor *did* say she didn't mind if we got a *bit* dirty," Bubble woofed, staring at it.

"Shall we?" Squeak barked naughtily.

They both turned round. Mary and her mum and dad were watching.

"We'd better not," Bubble yapped.

"All right, then," Squeak barked back. "We'll save it till tomorrow!"

Banger and Mash

To Norma, Rachel and Jade – with love and thanks

Chapter One

"Banger! Mash! You're very quiet up there. I hope you're not doing anything naughty?"

The two brown-and-white terrier pups looked at each other when they heard their owner's voice.

"No, Linda!" Banger barked. He

dropped Bob's slipper, which he had almost chewed to pieces.

"No, Linda!" woofed Mash. He had been happily chewing the other slipper to shreds.

"I think we'd better go downstairs," Banger yapped. He nudged what was left of Bob's slippers under the bed out of sight.

"It was *your* idea to chew Bob's slippers, Banger," Mash yapped back. "You said it would be a really good game."

"It *is* a good game," Banger woofed, "as long as Bob and Linda don't find out."

Quickly the two puppies trotted out of their owners' bedroom and across the landing. Just as they reached the top of the stairs, the doorbell rang.

"It's Mia!" Banger yelped in delight.

"Hang on, Mia," Mash barked urgently, "we're coming."

The puppies almost fell over each other as they scrambled down the stairs. Mia Smith and her mum had only been living next door for three weeks, but Mia had quickly become great friends with Banger and Mash.

Today Linda and Bob were going to visit Linda's mum, who lived a long way away. Banger and Mash had gone with them last time, but they'd found the car journey *very* boring. They'd whined and yapped so much that this time they were going to spend the whole day with Mia instead. And they were really looking forward to it.

"Be careful, you two," Linda laughed. As she came out of the living room, she almost tripped over the two excited pups.

"Quick, Linda," Banger and Mash barked together. "It's Mia!"

They raced down the hall in front of Linda, and waited impatiently for her to open the door.

Mia was standing outside. Banger and Mash rushed out to greet her.

"Hi, Mia," Linda said cheerfully. "Are you enjoying the school holidays?"

"Yes, thanks." Mia grinned at her. "Especially as it means I've got more time to play with Banger and Mash!"

"Stroke me first, Mia," woofed Banger, who was dancing around her ankles.

"No, *me* first," woofed Mash. He jumped up and pawed at Mia's knees.

Mia smiled and bent down to pick the two pups up. Banger and Mash took it in turns to cover her face with kisses. "I *did* have a bath today, boys," Mia laughed, hugging them both.

"It's really good of you to have the pups for us, Mia," Linda said gratefully. "I know you and your mum must be very busy decorating your bedroom."

"Decorating?" woofed Banger, cocking his head to one side. He looked across at Mash. "Mia and her mum are doing some decorating!"

"Brilliant," Mash barked. He wagged his tail so hard, it looked as if it might fall off. "We can help them, just like we helped Bob and Linda decorate the living room last week."

"Are you *sure* the pups won't be in your way?" Linda asked doubtfully. "They were quite a handful when Bob and I were painting our living room last week."

Mia laughed. "I'm sure they'll be OK," she said.

"Of course we will," Banger yapped indignantly.

"Yes, just wait till you see what we can do with a pot of paint, Mia," Mash yapped proudly. "You won't believe it."

"Linda, are you ready to go?" Bob came out of the kitchen, pulling on his coat. "We've got a long drive ahead of us." He grinned when he saw Mia. "Hi there, Mia. Thanks for looking after these two little terrors!"

"We're not terrors – we're terriers," yapped Mash crossly.

Banger and Mash followed Mia next door, while Bob carried over a bag of toys and their drinking-bowls. Then Mia and the puppies stood on the doorstep to wave goodbye.

"Be good, you two," Linda called, as she and Bob climbed into their car.

"Of course we will," Banger woofed.

After Linda and Bob had driven off, Mia took the puppies inside and closed the door.

There was a lot of banging and thumping going on upstairs in the Smiths' house.

Mia's mum appeared at the top of the stairs, looking very red in the face. "Put the pups in the kitchen, and come and help me, Mia," she called. "I can't move your bed on my own."

"Hello, Mrs Smith," Banger yapped, as Mia took them down

the hall to the kitchen. "Don't worry – we'll help with the decorating."

" Yes, we've had lots of practice," Mash woofed proudly.

But then Mia shut the kitchen door on them and ran upstairs!

The two pups sat down, disappointed.

"Oh, well," Banger sniffed. "I'm

sure Mia and Mrs Smith will come and get us to help them before long. Then we'll show them what to do."

Chapter Two

A few minutes later, Mia and her mum came into the kitchen.

"Oh, is it time for us to help now?" woofed Banger, his tail wagging.

But Mrs Smith just smiled and opened the back door. "Come on, you two," she said. "You can play in the garden while Mia and I get on with the painting. We don't want you getting under our feet."

Banger and Mash looked at each other, puzzled.

"But we want to *help*," Mash woofed.

"Yes, we're *brilliant* at decorating," yapped Banger.

"I don't think they want to go, Mum," Mia said, trying not to laugh.

"They'll be fine outside," Mrs Smith replied. "It's a nice warm day, and there's plenty of shade out there if they get too hot." She beckoned to the pups. "Come on, out you go."

Banger and Mash didn't move.

"Out!" said Mrs Smith firmly,

pointing at the garden.

"No-o-o-o-o-o," both puppies
howled dismally. And they sat
down on the kitchen floor and
refused to budge.

In the end, Mia had to pick them
up, one under each arm, and
carry them outside.

Mrs Smith followed with bowls of water and the bag of toys. Seeing the pups' miserable faces, she gave them a pat. "Never mind," she said. "We'll take you for a nice walk in the park when we've finished the painting." Then she stared from one to the other. "Goodness," she said to Mia. "They're so alike! How do you tell them apart?"

"That's easy," Mia said. "Banger has bigger patches of brown on his face – oh, and two dots on his nose."

"That's right, Mia," yapped Banger and Mash together. "Well spotted!"

Mia gave them a cuddle, then put them down on the lawn.

"Now be good, you two," she said. Then she and her mum hurried back into the house.

Banger and Mash were disgusted. They slumped down on the grass, their ears droopy and their noses between their paws.

"It's not fair," Banger sniffed crossly.

"Tell you what," Mash yapped, his tail beginning to wag a little. "Let's try to get back into the house. Then we can *show* Mia and her mum just how good we are at decorating."

Banger's ears perked up. "How?" he asked.

Mash bounded over to the flower bed next to the back door.

"We can dig a tunnel into the kitchen." He began to scrabble about, sending dirt flying in all directions. "Come on, Banger!"

Banger hurried to join him, and the two pups began to dig furiously. Soon they'd dug quite a big hole.

"Are we any closer to the house yet, Mash?" Banger panted. He

shook the dirt from his brown-and-white coat.

"Not yet," Mash puffed. "Keep digging."

Suddenly the pups heard the sound of Mia's bedroom window being flung open. They looked up and saw Mrs Smith leaning out. She had a paintbrush in her hand and she was wearing a big shirt streaked with yellow paint.

"Banger! Mash!" Mrs Smith shouted crossly. "Stop digging up my roses."

The two pups crept away from the flower bed with their tails between their legs. They slumped down on the grass again.

"Why is Mrs Smith being so mean?" Banger grumbled.

"I bet Mia would let us help," Mash agreed glumly.

The puppies looked at each other. Then they both threw back their heads and began to howl. "Mi-aaaaa! Mi-aaaaa! *Please* let us come in and help."

This time Mia opened the bedroom window and looked down at them. "Be quiet, boys!" she called. "Mum says you have to stay outside, and that's that."

Gloomily, Banger and Mash gave up. They could see that there was no way they were going to be allowed inside the house.

"I hope Mia and Mrs Smith know what they're doing," Banger woofed.

Mash yawned widely. "I'm a bit

sleepy. I'm going to have a nap
while we're waiting." He curled
up in the shade underneath one
of the trees.

But Banger didn't feel sleepy at
all. He played with his favourite
rubber bone for a while. Then he
began to nose around the lawn.

Soon he picked up a very

interesting smell. Banger knew exactly who it was – Fluffy, the big ginger cat who lived in a house across the road. To their disgust, Banger and Mash had once even seen Fluffy in Linda and Bob's garden. But they'd soon chased her out.

"Grr!" Banger growled softly, deep in his throat. "Don't you *dare* come near Mia's house, Fluffy!"

He followed the smell right to the bottom of the garden. *Maybe Fluffy is hiding down there somewhere*, Banger thought hopefully. If she was, he'd chase her all the way back to her own house.

But suddenly Banger forgot all about the big ginger cat. The large shed at the bottom of the Smiths'

garden was standing open.
Banger's shiny brown eyes lit up.
The pups had wanted to look
inside the shed since the Smiths
moved in, but the door had
always been closed.

"Mash!" Banger barked loudly.
"Wake up!"

Mash opened an eye. "Go away,
Banger," he growled. "I'm
asleep."

"The shed door's open," Banger
woofed. "And I'm going in."

"Really?" Mash jumped to his
paws, his tail wagging hard.
"Brilliant!" He dashed over to his
brother.

The two pups raced inside the
shed and looked around eagerly.
They found old furniture, garden

tools and cardboard boxes, as well as *lots* of interesting smells.

"There's loads of things to play with in here," Mash yapped happily. He attacked an empty cardboard box and began to tear it to bits.

But Banger wasn't listening. He was staring up at a shelf high above their heads. "Look, Mash," he woofed.

Mash glanced up at the shelf. All he could see on it were a couple of tins of paint. "Come and help me kill this cardboard box," he barked. "It's much more interesting."

"No, you don't understand," Banger woofed, nipping at his brother's tail. "We can use that paint up there to decorate the shed. *Then* Mia and Mrs Smith will see just how good at painting we are!"

Chapter Three

Mash cocked his head to one side. "That's a brilliant idea, Banger," he barked. "Except for one thing . . ."

"What?" Banger snapped impatiently.

"How are we going to get the paint down?"

"Oh, that's easy," Banger woofed. "I'll climb up onto that table underneath the shelf, and then I'll be able to reach the paint. Simple!"

"And how are you going to get up onto the table?" Mash asked.

"I'll climb onto the chair that's next to it," Banger replied.

"And how are you going to get up onto the chair?" Mash wanted to know.

"I'll climb up that big pile of flowerpots," Banger yapped. "Just watch me."

The plastic flowerpots were stacked up in a higgledy-piggledy way next to the chair. Banger began to climb up them. But as he crept higher, the pile of pots

began to sway from side to side rather alarmingly.

"Look out, Banger!" Mash barked anxiously.

Luckily, Banger managed to scramble safely onto the chair before the stack collapsed. Flowerpots flew everywhere. One of them landed right on top of Mash.

"Help!" Mash barked, running around the shed with the pot stuck over him like a snail shell. "Everything's gone dark."

"Stop running about," Banger woofed crossly as he climbed onto the table. "You're distracting me."

Mash managed to shake the flowerpot off at last. "Don't knock anything else over, Banger," he ordered, as his brother began to climb again.

The table was covered with gardening tools and packets of seeds. As Banger heaved himself up onto it, he knocked some of the packets to the floor. One of them was open, and seeds showered around Mash like noisy little raindrops.

"Banger!" Mash yelped crossly, as the seeds stuck to his fur. "Look what you've done." He shook himself hard to get the seeds out of his coat.

"Sorry," Banger woofed. He was standing on the table now. By stretching up on his short hind legs, he could just about reach the shelf with his front paws.

Puffing and panting, Banger scrambled up onto the narrow ledge. "I did it!" he barked triumphantly. "Look at me, Mash!"

"Yes, but what are you going to do *now*?" Mash asked. "How are you going to get the paint down?"

"Leave it to me," Banger barked

importantly. "Stand clear, Mash!"

And he gave the first tin a gentle
nudge with his nose. It moved
slowly forward, teetered on the
edge of the shelf for a moment,
and then fell towards the floor.
But, as it fell, the tin hit the table.
The lid shot off and bright blue
paint flew *everywhere*.

Everything in the shed was

splashed with paint – including Mash.

"*Banger*!" Mash howled, staring down at his coat. "I'm *blue*!"

But Banger was too busy nudging the other tin off the shelf to listen. The second tin flew down. As it hit the floor it exploded. And pale green paint covered the floor – *and* Mash.

"Now I'm blue *and* green!" Mash barked.

Banger looked down at his twin. "Hey!" he barked. "That looks great. Now it's *my* turn." He scrambled down, and . . . SPLAT! Banger launched himself into a blue paint puddle, then he ran over and rolled in the green puddle. Soon he was as blue and

green as his twin.

"Wheeee!" Mash barked happily, as he skidded along the floor, spraying paint in all directions. "Decorating the shed is fun!"

"Who needs paintbrushes?" Banger woofed. "We can just use our tails." He wagged his tail at his brother, flicking spots of paint everywhere.

"And our paws!" added Mash. He started jumping around. His paws left blue-and-green prints all over the wooden floor. "Mia and her mum will *have* to let us help them now."

The pups were enjoying themselves so much that they didn't hear footsteps coming closer to the shed. Suddenly, the door opened wide.

"*Oh!*" Mia gasped. "Banger and Mash, what have you *done*?"

Chapter Four

Banger and Mash looked around
and wagged their blue-and-green
tails proudly.

"Hello, Mia!" they woofed
together. "We *told* you we were
brilliant at decorating."

Mia just stood there with her
mouth open. She stared at the two

blue-and-green puppies, and the paint-covered shed. She was so shocked, she couldn't say anything.

"Look, Mia really likes it," yapped Banger. He playfully nipped his brother's blue left ear. "She likes it so much she can't think of a thing to say!"

"Yes," Mash agreed. "I knew she would. And maybe Mia's left the back door open," he woofed. "This could be our chance to help with her bedroom too."

Banger wagged his green-spotted tail. "Let's go for it!" he barked.

The two pups charged out of the shed and up the garden towards the back door. To their delight,

Mia *had* left the back door open.

"Come back, you two!" Mia shouted, racing after them. But she couldn't help laughing as she watched two blue-and-green bottoms bouncing up the garden.

"Sorry, Mia, can't stop," Banger panted.

"We've got some decorating to

do," Mash puffed. They hurtled into the house at top speed.

"Stop!" Mia yelled. "Mum will go mad if you get paint all over the house."

But it was too late. Banger and Mash raced through the kitchen and up the stairs, leaving blue-and-green pawprints on the wooden floors, all the way.

They ran into Mia's bedroom. Mrs Smith was standing on a stepladder painting a wall. She was concentrating so hard that she hadn't heard the puppies come up the stairs.

"Don't worry, Mrs Smith," Banger barked. "We're here to help now."

"That's not bad," Mash woofed

approvingly, as he looked at the yellow colour on the walls. "But we can make it even better!"

Mia's mum looked round, then gasped as she saw the green-and-blue pups. She almost fell off the stepladder. "Mia!" she shouted furiously. "What are Banger and Mash doing in here? And *why* are they all green and blue?"

Mia hurried into the room. "They were playing with some paint in the shed," she explained quickly.

"Not playing – *decorating*," Banger pointed out.

"And we don't need brushes either," Mash went on. "Look." And he gave himself a shake. Flecks of green and blue paint splashed over one of the yellow walls.

"Mia, look what they've done," Mrs Smith groaned.

"Yes, we're helping you decorate," Banger barked loudly, and he wagged his tail against another wall. A green-and-blue feather pattern appeared.

"Nice work, Banger," Mash yapped admiringly.

"Quick, Mia, catch them!" said Mrs Smith. She began to climb down the stepladder as fast as she could. But she wasn't looking where she was going. And when she reached the bottom, she put her foot onto the lid of the paint pot. "Oh, no!" she cried. She hopped around trying not to drip

yellow paint on the floor.

"You're not as good at decorating as we are, Mrs Smith!" Mash woofed. He and Banger ran around the room rubbing against the walls. They left a green-and-blue trail behind them.

"Get them out of here, Mia!" Mrs Smith shouted. Red-faced, and standing on one foot, she tried to clean her trainer.

Mia dashed over to the pups.
But Banger and Mash had come
to help decorate and they were
determined to finish the job.
Banger scampered in one
direction and Mash went off in
the other. Mia couldn't catch
either of them.

"We *told* you we were great at
decorating," Banger barked
proudly. He shook himself against
a patch of wall and added some
more brightly coloured specks.

"This is brilliant fun," Mash
woofed happily. He jumped up
and leaned on a wall with his two
front paws to add a few artistic
pawprints.

By now Mrs Smith had taken off

her paint-covered trainer, and was chasing after the puppies too. "Shut the door, Mia," she yelled, "so that the pups are trapped in here."

It wasn't so easy for Banger and Mash to avoid being caught now. A few moments later, Mia managed to pounce on Banger. She held him tight. Her mum grabbed Mash.

"Thank goodness!" Mrs Smith gasped. "Now let's get them out of here."

Mia stared hard at the puppy she was holding. Then she looked at the pup in her mum's arms. "Oh, dear," she said. "They're both so covered in paint, I can't tell which one's Banger and which one's Mash!"

"I'm Banger," woofed Banger, licking Mia's cheek.

"And I'm Mash," barked Mash from Mrs Smith's arms.

"It doesn't matter which one's which," said Mia's mum. She stared gloomily round the room. "Just *look* at the mess they've made."

Chapter Four

"What mess?" Banger and Mash
yelped. They were very surprised
– and a bit hurt too. After all their
hard work, the lower half of the
boring yellow room now had a
very interesting blue-and-green
pattern.

"Don't you like it, Mia?"

whimpered Mash, hanging his head.

"We were only trying to help," Banger whined. He buried his face in Mia's sweatshirt.

There was silence for a moment or two while Mia stared around her bedroom walls. Then, suddenly, her face split into a big grin. "But, Mum," she said, "it looks like one of those special paint effects from that TV programme – you know, the one where people decorate each other's rooms. And I *love* it!" she announced.

The puppies pricked up their ears. They both stared at Mia. Had she *really* said she liked it? Their tails gave a little wag.

Mrs Smith looked at the walls again. Finally, she said, "Mmm . . . yes . . . I see what you mean." And now she was smiling too.

The puppies' tails wagged like mad.

"Phew," woofed Banger. He gave Mia's chin a lick.

Mash couldn't reach Mia, so he gave her mum a lick instead.

"Well, I think that's *quite* enough excitement for one day," said Mrs Smith, laughing. "We'd better clean our two little artists up, before Linda and Bob get back."

Suddenly Mia looked worried. "Mum, what if the paint won't come off?" Then she gasped. "And what if it's *poisonous*? It might make Banger and Mash ill!"

Mrs Smith shook her head. "Don't worry, Mia," she said. "If they found it in the shed then it's the paint we used in the spare room. I know it's not poisonous, and it will wash off in water."

"Oh, good," said Mia, relieved.

"The sooner we get these two washed, the sooner we can start to clean up in here, and in the shed. I dread to think what a state it's in. Here, Mia, take this one too," said her mum, handing Mash over. "I'll go and fill the bath."

Banger and Mash looked at each other in disgust.

"Huh!" grumbled Banger. "I'd rather be blue and green than have a bath!"

"Me too," Mash agreed gloomily.

Just then, the doorbell rang. Mrs Smith went down to answer it.

In a few moments, she returned – with Linda and Bob!

Chapter Six

"Oh!" Mia cried. "Hello. You're back early."

Linda and Bob smiled and nodded.

"When we got there, my mum was out," Linda explained. "She must have forgotten we were visiting."

Then their smiles faded as they saw the blue-and-green puppies tucked under Mia's arms.

"Is that Banger and Mash?" Linda gasped.

Bob stared at the pups as if he couldn't believe his eyes.

"Yes, it is," Mia admitted, feeling very embarrassed.

But Banger and Mash weren't embarrassed at all. They were wagging their sticky blue-and-green tails very happily.

"Hello, Linda," Banger barked proudly. "We've been doing some more decorating."

"Hi, Bob," Mash woofed. "What do you think of it? Nice, eh?"

Quickly Mia explained what had happened. Bob and Linda were

very apologetic then, after a minute, they both roared with laughter. "They just love messing about with paint," Linda said, pulling Mash's blue ears affectionately.

"We weren't messing about," Mash replied crossly. "We were *decorating*."

Just then, Banger's tummy rumbled. "And after all that hard work, we're starving," he added.

"We were just about to give the puppies a bath," said Mia.

Banger and Mash both started to wriggle. "Can't you feed us first?" they whined.

"I know that sound," Linda said with a grin. "They're hungry. We'd better feed them first, or they'll wriggle too much for us to bath them properly." She rolled up her sleeves and reached out to take Banger from Mia. Then she frowned, staring hard at the puppy. "Hang on a minute, which one is this? Banger or Mash?"

"It's me, Banger, of course," Banger snuffled indignantly.

"I don't know," Mia admitted anxiously. "I can't tell them apart now."

"Don't worry, Mia," Bob said. He grinned. "I know how to sort them out. Let's all go next door and I'll show you."

Linda winked at Bob. Then she turned to Mia. "I think Bob has a *special* supper in mind for Banger and Mash," she said.

Bob nodded, then led the way next door.

"A special supper!" yapped Banger excitedly.

"Linda and Bob must be really pleased with our decorating," woofed Mash from Mia's arms.

Next door, Mia and her mum followed Linda and Bob into the kitchen.

"I wonder how Linda and Bob will tell Banger and Mash apart when they are still covered in paint?" Mia said.

"I was wondering that too," yapped Mash. "My face is still green!"

"Well, we'll soon find out," said her mum.

Bob and Mrs Smith put plenty

of newspaper down in the kitchen, then Linda and Mia put the two sticky pups down on the floor.

Banger and Mash watched Bob go to the big white fridge in the corner and open its creaky door.

"I love that noise!" barked Mash, his tail wagging madly. It often meant little treats were on the way. And sometimes a delicious supper of leftovers from Linda and Bob's dinner.

"Me too," woofed Banger.

The two pups leaped around each other in excitement as Linda put one red and one blue food bowl on the worktop.

Bob took two foil-covered dishes out of the fridge. He peeled off

the foil and emptied each dish
into the food bowls. Banger and
Mash jumped up to see what he
was going to give them.

"Can you see what it is,
Banger?" barked Mash.

"Not yet," woofed Banger. He
nudged Bob's leg with his nose
and left a smudge of green
paint.

"Hey, Banger *or* Mash," said Bob with a grin. "Don't cover *me* in paint too."

"I'm Banger, and I just want to know what we are having for supper," yapped Banger.

"It's ready now, boys," said Bob, putting the food bowls on the kitchen floor. "Eat up quickly before all that paint dries, or we'll never get it off."

Mia was very surprised to see that the blue bowl was filled with bits of cold sausage, and the red bowl was filled with mashed potato.

"Yippee!" Banger barked happily, rushing towards the blue bowl. "Sausages – my favourite."

"Hurray!" Mash woofed, charging over to the red bowl. "Mashed potato – *my* favourite!"

The hungry pups buried their noses in the bowls, and started eating happily.

Mia began to laugh. "So *that's* why they're called Banger and Mash!" she exclaimed. "We

wondered why they had such funny names, didn't we, Mum?"

Mrs Smith nodded. She was laughing too.

"Of course, they don't get sausages and potatoes *every* day," Bob said with a grin. "But luckily, we had some left over from last night – which is just as well. They'll need their favourite treat before being scrubbed in the bath."

Mash looked up from his bowl. "Of course we do," he barked. "We worked really hard decorating Mia's bedroom."

"That's right," yapped Banger. "It isn't easy when you have to use your tail *and* paws."

"I hope they didn't cause too much trouble," Linda said to Mia and her mum. "Bob and I will come over later and help you clean up."

Then she turned to Mia. "Are you sure you like your walls with green and blue splashes?" she asked doubtfully.

"Oh, yes," Mia said firmly. "And once the new carpet's down, it will look great. We won't be able to see the pups' pawprints on the floor – or Mum's trainer-marks either!"

"In fact I might even decorate my bedroom tomorrow in the same colours," Mrs Smith added.

Banger stopped eating, and pricked up his ears. "Did you

hear that, Mash?" he barked. "We're decorating Mrs Smith's room next."

"Oh, brilliant," Mash woofed. "Eat up all your sausages, Banger – we're going to be working hard again tomorrow!"